Wolf Hill

Dirt Bike Rider

Gizmo's Story

D0555668

Roderick Hunt

Illustrated by Alex Brychta

OXFORD
UNIVERSITY PRESS

OXFORD
UNIVERSITY PRESS

Great Clarendon Street, Oxford, OX2 6DP

Oxford   New York
Athens   Auckland   Bangkok   Bogotá   Buenos Aires   Calcutta
Cape Town   Chennai   Dar es Salaam   Delhi   Florence   Hong Kong
Istanbul   Karachi   Kuala Lumpur   Madrid   Melbourne   Mexico City
Mumbai   Nairobi   Paris   São Paulo   Singapore   Taipei   Tokyo
Toronto   Warsaw

and associated companies in
Berlin   Ibadan

Oxford is a trade mark of Oxford University Press

© text Roderick Hunt 1999
© illustrations Alex Brychta
First Published 1999

ISBN 0 19 918752 5

Printed in Hong Kong

Chapter 1

The bike roared up the hump. At the top, it took off. For a second it seemed to hang in the air. Then it landed on the track and raced away.

Close behind it were two more bikes; then four more. They all leaped high in the air. The noise was terrific.

'Brilliant!' shouted Gizmo.

Gizmo's dad was up a ladder. He was clipping a cable to a tall pole. 'Hey, Matthew,' he called. 'I thought you were helping. Pass up some cable clips.'

'Sorry,' said Gizmo. 'Did you see how high those bikes jumped?'

Mr Harding climbed down. 'Yes, and they're only practising. Wait until you see them race on Saturday.'

Mr Harding was putting speaker cable all round the track. 'There's just one more speaker to do,' he said.

A rider walked past pushing his bike. He was covered in mud. So was the bike.

'Trouble?' asked Mr Harding.

'My throttle stuck,' said the rider. I couldn't kill the revs. In the end I had to pull the carb's choke to shut off.'

The rider looked at Gizmo. 'Do you want a job? Come and hose my bike down. I'll show you what to do.'

Gizmo grinned. 'Sure!' he said. He looked at Mr Harding. 'Can I, Dad?' he asked.

'Well, OK,' said Mr Harding. 'Not every kid gets asked to hose down Paul Fox's LM 250.'

Chapter 2

Jools said he'd take Andy to the motocross on Saturday. Andy asked Gizmo if he wanted to come, too.

Gizmo said that he was already going. 'My dad worked on the sound system,' said Gizmo. 'I helped him.'

'Shall we meet you there, then?' asked Andy.

Gizmo couldn't help showing off. 'I can't,' he said. 'I've got a job there. I'm hosing down bikes for the Paul Fox Team.'

'I don't believe you,' said Andy.

It was true. Gizmo had done a good job on the LM 250 so Paul Fox had asked him to help on the race day. 'It's going to be muddy,' he said. 'If you want to hose down some bikes, the job's yours.'

Jools took Andy, Kat and Arjo.
They had never been to motocross
racing before. They were all excited.

They found Gizmo hosing down a
bike. He was using a power hose.

'Oh wow!' said Andy. 'Hey Gizmo!
Let me have a go.'

Gizmo went on hosing 'I can't,' he
said. 'There's a special way of doing
it.'

Andy walked away. He felt angry
with Gizmo. 'He's just a show-off. I
used to stick up for him. Now I wish
I hadn't.'

Jools put his hand on Andy's arm.
'Hey! Come on, Andy. Don't be
jealous.'

'I'm not jealous!' said Andy, angrily.
'Come on, let's watch the racing.'

Chapter 3

Andy spotted a section of fence on a sharp bend in the track. No one was standing by it.

'It's a great place to stand,' said Andy. 'We can watch them go up the hill.'

They soon found out why nobody stood there. The first bikes raced to the corner. The riders braked. They slid their back wheels into the bend. Then they opened their throttles to take the hill.

The back wheels kicked and spun.
Mud flew up from the track. It
splattered against the fence. Some hit
Jools in the chest. Some hit Arjo on
the forehead.

'Hey!' said Kat. 'Whose idea was it
to stand here? I've got mud in my
hair.'

Jools laughed. 'Come on,' he said. 'We'll need Gizmo to hose us down if we stand here.'

They found a place to watch at the top of the slope. The bikes flew through the air.

'It's spectacular,' said Andy. 'They must be two metres off the ground.'

Arjo took his deaf aids out. The noise was too loud for him.

A little while later, they saw Gizmo. He was by himself. He looked miserable.

'What's up?' asked Andy. 'Did you get the sack?'

'In a way,' said Gizmo. 'Paul Fox's son, Peter, turned up. He wanted to do the hosing down.'

'Well, you can watch the racing with us,' said Kat.

Chapter 4

Two weeks later, Paul Fox called at Mr Harding's shop. He looked serious. 'It's about that sound system you installed at the moto park.'

'There's nothing wrong, is there?' asked Mr Harding.

'Well, yes and no,' said Paul Fox. 'The moto park is new. It's cost a lot to set up. The problem is, we've run out of money.'

Mr Harding frowned. 'What are you saying? That you can't pay me?'

'Well, we can if you wait for your money. Or there's another way. I've got a junior bike and all the gear. It's an 80cc QX. It was my son, Peter's, but he's grown out of it. You could have the bike as payment.'

Mr Harding rubbed his chin. 'I don't know,' he said.

'I thought it would suit your boy. It's the right size for him. He can have the boots, the leathers, the gloves – everything. He could ride in junior events.'

Mr Harding looked thoughtful. He knew that Gizmo wasn't good at sport. Sometimes his asthma was bad. Maybe the bike would be good for him.

'I'll throw in a brand new crash helmet,' said Paul Fox.

'All right, it's a deal,' said Mr Harding. The two men shook hands.

After Paul Fox had gone Mr Harding gulped. 'What have I done?' he said. 'I don't even know if Gizmo wants a dirt bike.'

Chapter 5

Gizmo leaped to his feet. He gave a whoop and punched the air. His eyes shone with excitement. 'Oh, Dad, that's brilliant!' he said.

Gizmo's mum looked shocked. 'You've done what?' she exclaimed.

'I've got an 80cc dirt bike for Matthew, with all the gear,' repeated Mr Harding. He told them about the deal he had done with Paul Fox.

Mrs Harding sighed. 'Well, I hope Matthew takes to it,' she said, 'and I hope it's not dangerous.'

'Oh Mum!' said Gizmo. 'Lots of kids race dirt bikes. There are trials for boys and girls. I really, really want to do it.'

'All right,' said Mrs Harding. 'But I think we should go and see the bike. How do we know if it's any good?'

'I didn't think of that,' said Mr Harding. 'We'll go and see it this evening.'

'Brilliant!' said Gizmo.

Chapter 6

Gizmo kicked down on the gear lever. Then he twisted the throttle and let out the clutch. The bike reared forward and stalled.

'Let the clutch out slowly,' yelled Paul Fox. 'Don't give it too many revs.'

Gizmo tried again. This time, he got it right. The bike picked up speed.

Gizmo pulled in the clutch and
kicked it into second gear. The bike
leaped forward, but Gizmo slowed
the revs. His heart raced as he found
third gear – then fourth.

'Matthew! Not too fast,' yelled Mr
Harding. But Gizmo didn't hear. He
rode round the field three times.
When he tried to change down, the
bike stalled again.

'That was good,' said Paul Fox.
'How did it feel?'

'It was ace!' said Gizmo.

'Come and look at the gear,' said
Paul Fox.

He showed Gizmo the leathers and
boots. Gizmo tried them on. They
were a good fit.

'This is for protection,' said Paul
Fox. 'There are knee guards, elbow
pads and chest armour.'

Mr Harding grinned. 'I can see him racing, soon,' he joked.

'No reason why not,' said Paul Fox.

Mrs Harding had a thought. 'Where can Matthew learn to ride?' she asked.

'I'll tell you what,' said Paul Fox. 'You look after the sound system. I'll let you use this place for Matthew to practise.'

'It's a deal,' said Mrs Harding.

Chapter 7

Gizmo learned quickly. His mum and dad were pleased. 'It's good to see him enjoying it so much,' said Mrs Harding. 'Maybe he's found a sport he can do well at.'

'He's like a different boy,' said Mr Harding. 'He seems more sure of himself.'

It was true. Gizmo was different. He was good on the dirt bike. He soon learned to handle it. He began to try harder and harder things.

Peter Fox took him round the race circuit. 'It's about control,' he told Gizmo. 'You need to *feel* it. You have to be part of the bike. The bike has to be part of you.'

Peter Fox began slowly. As he went faster, so did Gizmo.

Mr Harding and Paul Fox watched them. 'Matthew is good,' said Paul Fox. 'I think he's a natural. How about putting him in for a race?'

'If he wants to,' said Mr Harding.

Paul Fox told Gizmo that there was a race meeting in a week's time. 'It's a club meeting,' he told Gizmo. 'Why don't you enter?'

Gizmo said he would. 'I won't come anywhere. I'll be lucky if I finish. But it will be good experience.'

That night Gizmo talked about the race. 'I can't wait to tell everyone at school,' he said.

As things turned out, he wished he hadn't.

Chapter 8

Gizmo told Andy that he was in a race. 'I've been doing OK,' he said. 'Paul Fox thinks I'm ready. Do you want to watch?'

Andy screwed his face up. 'No I don't want to watch you in a stupid race,' he said.

Gizmo blinked. It was not like Andy to be nasty.

'You're just a pain, Harding,' Andy went on. 'You're a show-off. You're always on about that stupid dirt bike.'

Gizmo was hurt. He looked at Andy through his misty glasses. 'I'm sorry,' he said.

'Who cares?' said Andy. As he walked away he said, 'And why don't you clean your stupid glasses?'

Late that evening, Jools went to see Mr Harding. 'It's about Andy and Gizmo,' said Jools. 'They've fallen out.'

'I know,' said Mr Harding. 'Matthew is quite upset about it.'

'The thing is,' went on Jools. 'I think Andy is jealous.'

'Jealous?' said Mr Harding. 'Why?'

'Andy has always stuck up for Gizmo,' said Jools. 'In the past, he's protected him. Now Gizmo has taken up dirt bike riding. He's good at it. Andy feels left behind. It makes him jealous.'

'I see,' said Mr Harding.

'Andy has no father,' said Jools. 'His mum and I are going out together and I try to help him if I can. I've had an idea.'

Jools paused.

'I want to get Andy a dirt bike.
How do I go about it?'

Chapter 9

It was the start of the race. Gizmo counted about twenty riders. He was at the end of the line.

It was not a good position. The first corner was a sharp left hander. The riders starting on the left had the advantage.

The orange flag went up. The bikes revved hard. They sounded like angry wasps. Blue exhaust smoke rose behind them.

Then they were off.

Gizmo went flat out for the first bend. He braked sharply, took it wide, then opened the throttle. It was a good tactic. It put him fifth in the field.

He slowed for the next bend. Two riders shot past him. Gizmo gritted his teeth. He had slowed too soon. That way he had let other riders through.

Now Gizmo was chasing the six riders. They were all good. They were pulling away from the others.

Gizmo set himself a challenge. He would stay with the six front runners. He would try to come in seventh.

After two laps he had caught up. He tried to get past the back rider. Every time he tried, the rider blocked him.

On the last lap, Gizmo saw his
chance. The rider went wide on the
final bend. Gizmo rode at the gap.
His handlebar clipped the other bike,
but he was through.

He had come in sixth.

Andy rushed up. 'Well done, Gizmo,' he said. 'I can't wait to get my bike, now.'

Gizmo grinned. 'I'm glad you decided to come,' he said.

It was good to have Andy back as a friend.

Chapter 10

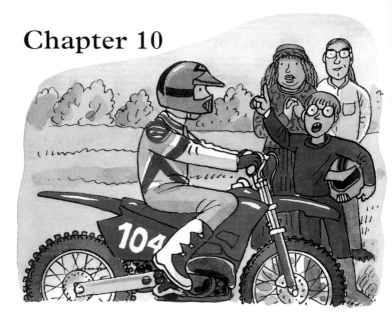

That week, Andy got his bike. It was a TZ 80.

'Let the clutch out gently,' said Gizmo. 'Twist the throttle slowly at first.'

Andy's mum looked nervous. 'Just be careful, Andy,' she called. 'I don't want you hurting yourself.'

Jools shook his head. 'He'll be OK,' he said.

It took Andy a long time to get going.

He kept stalling the bike. He began to get upset. 'I'll never get it right,' he said.

'Yes, you will,' said Gizmo. 'Don't give up.'

An hour later, Andy and Gizmo were riding round and round the field. Andy gave a 'thumbs-up'. It made him wobble a bit.

'Oh, be careful, Andy,' gasped his mum.

'Relax, Kim,' said Jools. 'You're making him nervous. What will you be like when he falls off?'

'I can't help it,' said Andy's mum.

Andy changed down and came to a stop. Gizmo pulled up behind him.

'It's just great,' said Andy. 'I can't wait to go racing.'

'You'll have to practise a bit first,' said Gizmo.

Chapter 11

Andy and Gizmo practised all summer. Soon, Andy was going round the track. He did well, but he couldn't ride like Gizmo.

One day, Gizmo told Andy to chase him. Every time Andy got close, Gizmo would pull away. Andy had to admit it. Gizmo was good.

The difference between them was that Gizmo felt he had to win. Andy didn't care about winning. In his first race, he came second last.

'Dirt bikes are fun,' Andy told himself, 'but I'm not cut out for racing.'

All the same, Andy was pleased for Gizmo. He had found a sport he was good at.

The next race was a big one. It was the Club Championship. Jools wanted Andy to enter. 'Just have a go,' Jools said. 'No one expects you to win.'

Andy didn't tell Jools that he wasn't keen on racing. He felt he had to enter to please Jools.

Gizmo was pleased. The race was at the moto park. 'I'm on home ground,' he said. 'I know every twist and bump.'

As things turned out, Gizmo almost didn't race. Someone tried to wreck his chances before the race started.

Chapter 12

Gizmo's parents took their caravan to the race meeting. They could have a meal in it. Gizmo could change in it, or rest before the race.

Gizmo and Andy were in the caravan reading comics. Some boys were looking at his bike outside the caravan.

Gizmo glanced out of the window.
One of the boys was messing with his
bike. He was fiddling with the petrol
cap. Gizmo banged on the window
and the boys ran away.

Gizmo didn't think any more about
it. Kids often look at bikes at race
meetings. Sometimes they touch
them.

Then it was time for the race.

Gizmo and Andy got ready. They
put on their leathers and body
armour. Jools and Mr Harding
checked the bikes.

Andy was nervous, but Gizmo said,
'Just do the best you can.'

Gizmo tried to start his bike. The
engine fired up. Then it died. Gizmo
tried again. Nothing happened. Then
it backfired.

Mr Harding tried. The bike still wouldn't start. Gizmo thought back. He remembered the boy touching his petrol cap. 'I think my fuel has been spiked,' he said.

'I can't believe it,' said Mrs Harding. 'Why?'

'Someone doesn't want Gizmo to race,' said Jools.

Mr Harding made a face. 'I don't think we can fix it in time,' he said.

'Let Gizmo use my bike,' said Andy. 'He's ridden it before. I won't race. It's the only thing to do.'

Chapter 13

Gizmo lined up for the start on Andy's bike. It would be a tough race for him. He wasn't used to the TZ 80.

In a big race quite a few riders make mistakes. Mistakes cost places. Poor riders get in the way of good riders. Sometimes they take them out of the race. The early laps are the worst.

Gizmo decided on a race plan. He
would wait his time. He would move
up once the field was spread out.
That way he'd keep clear of trouble.

They were off! The riders charged
at the first corner. There was a tangle
of bikes. One rider stalled. Three
came off. Gizmo kept clear of
trouble. He tucked in behind the
leading twelve riders.

Two riders went wide on the third bend. Gizmo nipped past. Then came the steep hill. The TZ 80's throttle was easier than his QX. Andy's bike seemed to have more power. Gizmo passed another rider on the hill.

At the crest, Gizmo flew too high. He almost came off. But he was lucky. He landed well. He was now tenth. The race was going to plan.

Slowly he moved up. By the ninth lap he was in sixth place. The leading two riders crashed into one another. That put him fourth.

He stuck to the rider in third place, waiting for him to make a mistake. Then the rider's front wheel hit a rut. It gave Gizmo his chance.

Now Gizmo was lying third – and there were two laps to go.

Chapter 14

It was the last lap. Gizmo's heart pounded. He looked for a gap but the leading riders were too good. However hard Gizmo tried he couldn't get past. The chequered flag went up. Gizmo had come third.

'Fantastic!' said Mrs Harding. She smacked Jools so hard on the back, his sunglasses shot off.

'Well done,' said Jools. 'You rode well.'

'Where's Andy?' asked Gizmo. 'Didn't he watch the race?'

'He's been doing some detective work,' said Jools. 'We think he's spotted the boy who spiked your fuel.'

Paul Fox sent for Gizmo. In his office were two boys. 'Are these the boys you saw messing with your bike?' he asked.

Gizmo nodded.

Paul Fox looked serious. 'Well, leave me to deal with them,' he said. 'They spiked three bikes. They were trying to fix the race.'

Gizmo went and found Andy.
'Thanks, Andy,' he said. 'Thanks for lending me your bike. Thanks for helping to catch those kids.'

'All part of the service,' said Andy. 'After all, what are friends for?'